A True Fan Girl

ALEENA E V

Made with ❤ on the Notion Press Platform

www.notionpress.com

Dedicated to my mother who is nothing like Crystal's mother.
And to all my dear fellow ARMYs

Contents

Foreword

I am super excited to write the foreword for this book as this is my first foreword and this is the first book from the author herself.

What can I tell about Aleena, the young author is so passionate about writing and she wants to make some impact on this world. She is a warrior herself and this book is a fantastic piece that has come out of her.

The story revoles around a fan girl crystal, her challenges and how her idol helps her in overcoming life challenges. I am sure that many of the young readers would be able to relate to crystal and her struggles. Nobody knows what other people are going through in their life. However, by being authentic and being always open to receiving as well as giving, we do not know how we will touch other's life.

This book will be a good read for all the teenagers and parents out there.

Deepa Joseph

Mother of the young author Aleena

08 January 2024

Preface

The story follows a girl named Crystal Kim from Busan and all the struggles she goes through in her teenage life, where she meets an idol who changes her life.

This story is based on my true feelings for the well-known idol Taehyung Kim. Though the incidents and other characters are fictional, i could relate to Crystal as a fan girl. Because all we fan girls do does recieve hate for liking someone who actually made an impact on our lives without them even know.

Aleena E V

08 January 2024

Acknowledgments

My family whom i hold close to my heart and my best friend Saniya Bylon who supported me through each stage as i wrote this book

1. The Days of Struggle

As I lay down all I could see was the ceiling of my room. My vision blurred with my tears and the sound of heavy rain filled the air. There were books scattered all around me and I could barely breathe. I imagined myself in front of all those people who were staring at me and laughing at my failure. A sudden thought of death came over me.

[Flash back]

I was that girl who never talked to anyone at school. The one who was in her own world having her nose deep in a book. I scored good marks as well. However, I mostly preferred my own company. No one at school cared about my existence and I learned to like it. Unlike others, I already had a plan about my future since my young age - ART. Art was always my passion and I thus wanted it to be my profession as well. Of course, no one in my family took it seriously and I was off to study business. To be honest, I hated every minute of it. My parents felt that art would never get me anywhere in life. Rest of my relatives supported that decision.To many, studying business at one of the biggest universities would be a dream come true but for me it was living hell.

Once I sneaked my sketchbook to my room so I could catch up on drawing again. However, my parents found out and all my art supplies were confiscated. If that was not enough now I had to work part time at a diner to pay my fees. Working late nights and running errands for the diner always made me so tired that I would sometimes miss a few classes in the morning. My parents would get furious and ask the diner owner not to pay me that week. This went on until the last year of my studies. In addition, it was hectic.

Soon came the finals and the interviews and I scored pretty good marks this time as well, although I wasn't glad, I made it in the top ten highest rank holders. My parents were proud.Next was the interviews, which I was scared off. I entered the room to find three men and two women all dressed in black ready to interview me.

Then after a quick introduction as fast as lightning came questions from all of them but I could hear my heart pounding as I noticed the look on their faces after each of my answers. Being an introvert seemed to take a bad turn and before I could say anything more, I felt myself falling down a deep black void.

"Is she alright?" my mother's words awoke me. I looked around I was not dreaming I was in a hospital. I had fainted. "You are awake" my dad said, the next thing I knew was my mother's hand on my face. "How could you do this to us" she scowled at me. Her eyes were red but not from tears of love, she was not worried about my health but about the interview. "You failed, how could you? You are a disgrace to our family" she took me by the collar and was ready to fling her hands at me. However, my dad stopped her just in time or I would have been unconscious again. “Not now honey, we’ll deal this back home he said grabbing a hold of her fist.

Back home my day got even worse than you could imagine, my parents were furious and I could see shocked faces around. A grin appeared on my sibling’s faces and I saw my uncles and aunts laughing from the corner of my eye. “Oh no we are so sorry” some of them said to my parents but not out of sympathy but of happiness that a girl who got to study at a top university failed in life.

This was just the beginning of the storm. After all my relatives had left the house, the real storm started. “Go to your rooms” my mom, ordered my two younger siblings while the other two stayed for the show. “Do you have any idea what you have done? You are a disgrace to the family name,” she screamed. “But mom…” before I could say anymore a hit fell on my face causing me to fell down. My mother took a vase in her hand and threw it at me, I barely dodged it. It felt like she was about to kill me. “MOM” I screamed the top of my lungs. “STOP” I had enough bruises today and I was not going to let her hurt me anymore. “What did I do? Was it my fault? You always cared about yourself and never cared about me. Was it my idea to study this? NO, I never wanted it, you did, and you wanted me to study something I never cared about. You made me work late at night even when I was sick. And it was you who took away my art supplies that I cared about the most” another slap fell across my face.

“You disrespectful brat, how dare you speak up to me! Do you know how much money we spent on you, you know how much clothes and things we bought you, do you even know how much they cost". Her words showed that it was clearly about the money and not about me.

"Arrgh…" she let out a loud scream which would have probably woken up the people next door. "That's it, I have had enough of you" she went upstairs, and her stomping made it feel like the stairs would fall down any minute. She marched down with a bag and threw it at me. "Here, now get lost. I do not want to see your face ever again. From today, I will not have such a daughter.

What just happened, I could not believe my ears. Were they deceiving me? No, it was true my parents in fact disowned me. She pushed me out the front door and told me to get lost. She slammed the door at my face and did not care to look back.

A cold wind blew, and it started to rain out of nowhere. I walked a few distance until I caught a taxi, which took me to my hostel. The hostel was practically empty as everyone left for home after interviews. Only a few were seen around packing their things, getting ready to leave. I went back to my room.

[Present]

I lay on my bed crying as the thought of death slightly crossed my mind. A notification rung suddenly on my phone and caught my attention.It was about an old MV about the boyband BTS it was from their second mini album SKOOL LUV AFFAIR. It was titled JUMP. At first, I thought I should ignore it, but music as an art form always calmed me somehow.Though a bit hesitant I unlocked my phone and played the video. It was an upbeat song but the words immersed me into the song. Suddenly I heard a voice say "No matter who tries to stop me I will go on my way, you only live once, lets go lets go" I wiped away my tears to look, it was Taehyung's voice. Moreover, those words pulled me back to reality.

2. Voice of V

I pulled myself back up. Yes, he was right; I should not give up on myself. I will never be able to live another life again. V's words brought me a strange wave of courage. I packed up my books, albums, merch and a few sheets of paper, the money I made from working this week at the diner (which wasn't much, but it was better than nothing), rest of my clothes and left the place.

All I ever wanted was to live my life and somehow now was the best time to do that. I already had back all my art supplies when mom threw me out of the house. The thought of being able to draw again warmed my heart. That is because when one draws, they are completely transferred into the project they are working on. As an artist, (well I consider myself an artist) I actually have the freedom to create what I love, without the permission of anyone else. No one gets to judge me and even if someone does, I actually do not even have to care. Of course, there are downsides to being an artist, but at times, the small wins are all that matters. I booked a train ticket although I had no idea where to go. I hoped that life would somchow show me the way.

On the train, I reminded myself why I like V; it is because of his personality. He seems to be a unique person. In addition, from what I see, he sees things in a different way than others and wishes to express his feelings and emotions in a rather creative way.I loved Tata (BT21) for obvious reasons. However, even tata was unique from others and his heart shape head symbolises the love he wanted to give out into the world. Somehow, thinking about Taehyung made me forget all that happened today.

I took out my phone and earphones and started to rewatch ep 31 “The Variety Shows of Memories” part 2 of Run BTS. As I watched them play the “half asleep game” and them singing the “amazing tomato” song had me laughing so hard I could feel my stomach hurt (of course I laughed on the inside, I did not want to be thrown out of the train as well). As night approached quickly, I felt myself falling into a deep sleep on the train. You could say I fell asleep with BTS (cause they were really about half-asleep in ep 31)

I was awaken by rays of sunlight, which penetrated through the window of my compartment. “Oh it’s morning, wait, where am I “I murmured to myself as I woke up rubbing my eyes and letting out a yawn. I curiously looked around and saw people who where really excited to get down from the train. Then I heard a squeal from a group of girls from the seat behind me “We are in Seoul, yay”.

WHAT – my mind just stopped Seoul? But how could I be in Seoul! Though I was scared at first, my fangirl personality took the best of me. For a moment in life, I was scared and excited at the same time. I was actually at the place where aspiring artists come to chase their dreams.

Was this a coincidence or had thinking about BTS and V really brought me to the city of Seoul?

3. Magic of Seoul

As I got down and looked around, it felt like I was dreaming, maybe I am in a fantasy world I thought to myself. Nevertheless, the squeals and chatter from all around made it clear that I was in fact in Seoul. I could feel my heartbeat rise again.This time of happiness, maybe it was fate, maybe this would be a new beginning.

The streets were filled with colours one could not imagine. People smiling at each other and paying their respects.it felt so cheerful.I saw a little girl in a light pastel dress handing out flowers while greeting people to have a good day. Laughter of children playing filled the air. Happy faces were the only things I could see around. I wanted to stay there and soak in all the positivity but first I needed to find a place to stay and most importantly - A Job. I would not care if I were paid a very low wage. I just wanted to stand up on my own feet for once.

I walked down the streets as sun shined bright like Hobi's smile. The sky was very clear and beautiful unlike the day before. Maybe the world knew I would be better off here. As I was walking along the sidewalks reading articles on V something caught my attention.It was a grandmother trying to cross the road with two huge bags in each of her hands. Coincidentally or not the article I was reading had a sentence like this "This showed how good of a grandson he was". It was as if V was communicating to me through the article.

She was so cute, but she was having a bad time. I ran over and took one of the bags. "No no its fine" she said in a soft voice. "It's ok I rather feel happy helping you." Those words came out of my mouth so quickly that I was confused whether it was me who spoke. Although she insisted not to, I carried both the bags and guided her across the road. "Thankyou dear" she said as she patted my shoulder and reached for the bags. "I'm glad I could help you," I said. Suddenly I noticed something, her bags were actually filled with paint tubes. "Oh these are good." A voice came out of me. "Oh you know this brand?" she asked surprised. "Yes, I know it. It has always been one of my favourite brands to paint with, though it's cheap it has amazing quality.""Well I guess you do know these then" she smiled. I nodded in agreement.

"Where are you headed to grandma?" I asked out of curiosity. "To my studio down the block" she pointed to a distance. "And by the way you can call me Fei Fei" she chuckled. I found her too cute I could not stop myself from blushing. "I will help you till there" before she could answer back, I took one of the bags and skipped in the direction she pointed. I could hear her little laugh from behind me.

Once I reached the studio she directed me to, I was too tired carrying both my bag and hers. "Wait here" she told me as I sat down. Within a few minutes she came back out with a glass of cold lemon juice, it was so refreshing.

I do not know if it was because of all the work I had done but it was the best one I ever drank. “Thankyou” I said as I wiped my face after returning the glass. “What is your name dear?” she asked. “Crystal” I replied cheerfully. “So what do you do?” another question came from her. At first, this question made me want to leave the place, but I told her my story. “I’m so sorry honey,” she said as she slightly hugged me from the side. “So you draw? If you want to, I’d be glad to have you here in my studio.” I looked at her in surprize as she continued. “You know, you remind me of myself. I always dreamt of a career in art and thus opened this art studio. However, as times changed, business slowed down. That’s why it looks empty and abandoned.” She was right it looked as if no one had visited the place in years. “I’d be happy to help. But right now I need a place to stay” I said. “Oh that’s ok you can stay with me, I live alone, there will be plenty of space for you and I’ll give you your privacy.” Those words were good to hear. She sounded truthful, and who in their right minds would turn down a woman in their 80’s. “I’d love that and I’d be more than glad to help out with your studio” I exclaimed. Fei Fei let out a tiny squeal of happiness, which made both of us, giggle. I entered the art store and started to clean it up.

There were cobwebs and spiderwebs in every little corner. The paper was peeling off the wall. The shelves were in bad condition as well. But I knew now, there was no turning back. I was in it to win it, well more like in it to clean it. Through a lot more struggle, I was able to clean half of the room and shelves. Now there were boxes everywhere filled with art supplies, a huge stack of canvases on the floor and more dust than one can imagine. “That’s fine for today, lets go home and take rest okay” Fei’s words were just the thing I needed.

She took me home. It was a small cottage with greenery surrounding it everywhere. She showed me her cattle that grazed in a distance and took me in. Inside was cute and comfortable than you could imagine, it reminded me that even without a lot of money one could find happiness in the little things. Now that I had a place to stay, maybe I could start working on my dream. I knew it would be a rough start, but I wanted to try cause Taehyung once said, “don’t let your dreams just be dreams”.I relaxed for the rest of the day.

The next morning, I woke up at dawn. I wanted to surprise Fei Fei. I went up to her store and started painting a mural on the store walls up front. It was a way of me thanking her for everything she had done for me, but also in the back of my mind, I thought maybe it ‘d help bring in more customers. At about eight, she came up to me and squealed in happiness “Thank you it looks beautiful” her hug made me feel warm inside. It felt good. I would have been a great grandchild just like V, maybe I could be a good artist like him, of course not in music but with paints. “Can I paint on this canvas?” I asked her hopefully. “Of course you can” her words brought me joy.As I started painting, people started noticing the store and us, they started coming up to us getting interested. “Can I buy some of your works?” a lady said “Yeah me too” someone else said. “And me” voices kept on rising.

People wanted our work. And they even began to pay. “Customers” Fei said happily. Soon many of my new paintings and sketches had new homes. “I have a job!” I thought to myself. It felt amazing. Finally, I had a job even though it was not a big job, and I did not earn much, I made money off what I loved.

Thoughts of Taehyung had guided me to Seoul and made me help an old woman who provided a JOB and shelter. Maybe I am thinking too much but as a fan girl, I could feel him and his words guiding me to a much safer and happier life.

4. Stories of V

As days passed, studio became more beautiful, and my works improved in style and quality. I could now make prints and people actually bought them. God had made my life beautiful, and V was the guardian angel who chose to guide me through it. My struggles were now part of the past and something that I did not want to remember anymore. As months passed, my friendship with Fei Fei grew. She took me along to meet her friends. In addition, I would enjoy reading to 15 old women every day. Also, guess what, now all of them love K-pop and stan different groups. Its funny watching them arguing for their groups.

Once during our talk sessions, grandma Lee said, "My grand daughter said she was in love with V and no one else could have him" they all cackled. She then turned to me and asked, "You like him too right Crystal?" Are you like this too?" she laughed. Now there were many curious eyes focused on me. "No of course not, I mean I love him, but just as a fan, nothing more. And I don't mind other girls having him as their bias." I said. "So you don't plan on falling in love with him," grandma Lee said. I burst out laughing "Me – WHAT – Him – kekekeke" I could not stop laughing. I laughed so much that my stomach started to hurt. I got up and spoke, still laughing a bit "no way (keke still giggling) first it's not possible, and second, I told you I love him only as a fan nothing more. I looked at their faces after hearing no response to my words. They were all staring at me as if I got no jams. "You are the first girl I've ever heard say something like that," she said. I smiled at myself, I was proud. I think Fei Fei noticed I heard her giggle.

Over the days, we all would gather at each other's houses or at the common ground to talk and spend time together. Here is another such story that happened once.

One evening we were all eating gimpab and laughing at jokes. "So, how did your love for these boys (BTS) start?" asked Mrs. Choi unexpectedly. She was a retired schoolteacher. "Well, it was because of my best friend Esther" I replied. Everyone turned to me as I continued. "She actually became their fan since their debut, and once I heard a song of theirs while I was with her. It was called Dope, I loved everything about the song, the message, the dance moves, the beat, everything. As days passed, under her influence I found myself in love with them. "So, who is Esther? You've never told us about her." Fei said "Mhhm" the 15 women nodded in harmony. "Well, I'm sorry I didn't mention her before, but she is or well in this case was my best friend. We were classmates and thus friends since childhood. We were like V and Jimin, soulmates. We used to do everything together. Sing, dance, write, study, eat and even sleep. However, as times passed, I was forced to study business while she had to leave to another country to follow her dream. We still keep in touch every day. "So that's whom you talk to everyday on the phone?" asked Fei, "Yep that's her" I replied with a smile.

[Months Later]

On my birthday this year, I got the biggest surprise of my life – A Puppy!

All of them had saved up money over the past months and bought me not just any puppy, you guessed it, same as Tae, a Pomeranian. "Oh my god. Thank you thank you" I said as tears of joy rolled down my cheeks. "What will you name her?" someone from the crowd asked. "Everest (Evie)" I replied as I hugged her. Soon she became my full-time companion and bestie.

It has been 8 months since I arrived at Seoul. As more days passed, our business grew, now I made a decent amount from my artwork and the store was always filled with customers. I started receiving commissions and orders and I was happier than ever.

I wondered what would have happened if I had not chosen this path…?

5. Meeting my strength

[2 months later]

As the days went by the world became much prettier, it felt like I was living a dream. Evie and I became companions for life, she is now a very well trained pup. My entire past trauma had disappeared completely from my life. I was a new me.

"Ahhh" a scream startled me. I ran outside the store and there were many girls screaming their lungs out. "It's happening, omg its happening" "I can't believe this ahh" "My dreams are going to come true ahh" these screams filled the air. "What happened?" I asked one of the girls. "BTS is having a fan meet." She squealed, I almost lost my hearing. But I would not blame her. Because ahh this is happening for real. The boys are really having a fan meet. In addition, I can actually attend it.

It was on short notice, but they are having a fan meet in two weeks from now. That gave me enough time to prepare for it. I wanted to paint portraits as gifts for them.

[2 weeks later] Day of fan meeting

Finally, the day arrived. I was at the fan sign, I could not believe it. And as expected, being the biggest fandom in the world, the place was packed with people. Though there were many fans of the maknae line, I also spotted many fans of the Hyung line, it was heartwarming to see all the members receive equal and undying love.

Everything went by quick but the excitement of the crowd did not cease. Soon we were in line to get a chance to lock eyes with our 7 wonders of the world. There were about 15 people in front of me. But suddenly the lights went out. “Everyone please leave peacefully” I heard a sharp voice among the crowd. “There is a storm warning” said an officer. NO, this cannot be happening to me. Finally, after many years I had the chance to see them. I was so close to them, yet the world decided to shut itself on me again. I could feel tears running down my eyes, the members were escorted to safety and many of us had to be dragged away. It was heartbreaking.

However, it was for the best. As I was heading out, I saw a girl a bit younger than me, looking around confused. It seemed like she was lost. The first thought I had was to help her. I ran up to her. “Hi” I said, “Are you lost, may I help you?” I asked as I knelt down to her. She was cute as if she had come out of a cartoon. “Umm can you take me inside please? I forgot the way,” she said in a sweet tone. “Sure” I reassured her. While we were walking back inside, unexpectedly she asked, “Aren’t you sad you didn’t get to meet your idols?” “Its fine, they had to leave due to the emergency. I rather have them be safe than meet them. Who knows maybe I’ll get a chance one day again.” That is when I realised that I was not sad anymore. “You are so different from the others I saw” she said, “Many girls were running back really mad crying and screaming that they couldn’t meet the love of their lives" both of us couldn't hold back our laughter. "Maybe it's because I love them for them, I love them as idols and nothing more. I love everything about them but as an inspiration."

"Well thank you" a voice came from behind. It was so familiar. I turned around and it was V right there in front of me in real flesh. "Brother" the girl ran up to him that is when I realised why I thought the girl looked familiar. It was Tae's sister.

"Thank you for bringing my sister back safely" he said. "By the way I'm Taehyung and you?"

Ok I felt my spirit leave my body. "Hi I'm Crystal and yes I know who you are. And welcome" I mumbled to get my words right. That is when I saw six more people running up to us. You guessed it, it was the rest of the members. 'Who is she?" Hobi asked. Tae and his sister explained everything to them. The rain was pouring so much now, imagine being stuck in a hall with your idols. Yeah you are jealous; I get it I mean who would not be. "I guess we can't leave anytime soon," RM said looking outside. "True" Jimin said. "So tell us about yourself," JK said" Yes you did not get a chance to meet us then but here we are with all the time in our hands. It would be bad if we don't get to know at least one of our ARMY," said RM. "Yeah tell us about yourself" Jin and V said in harmony. "Don't be shy" said Yoongi. So I told them everything that happened, who I am where I came from. I even gave them the paintings I had done for each of them. "Wow you are strong," said an amazed Jin after hearing my story. “Don’t worry, everything will go great in the future” Jimin said with an angelic smile. “Yeah” the rest of the members said. “I’m glad I could be a pillar you could lean on when you needed the support and strength,” Tae said as he patted my hand. “We hope everything goes well and wish you more amazing things and success in life,” said Jhope. He really was a sun that brought life into a person.

Soon the weather calmed down and they were asked to leave so they could get some rest. Thus, we all said our goodbyes and parted ways.

.

.

Epilogue

A little bit of kindness brought me to V's sister, which in turn brought me to him and other members. I could feel my heart hitting hard against my chest. The rain slowly disappeared, and the sun shone bright again. Just like my life. From a dangerous storm to a bright blue sky, my life had changed so much. Moreover, along the way I had an idol whom I could lean on when I struggled the most. This was the new beginning of my life.

www.ingramcontent.com/pod-product-compliance
Lightning Source LLC
LaVergne TN
LVHW041302150826
845673LV00008B/2696

* 9 7 9 8 8 9 2 3 3 7 0 4 5 *